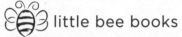 little bee books

An imprint of Bonnier Publishing USA
251 Park Avenue South, New York, NY 10010
Copyright © 2018 by Little Bee Books
All rights reserved, including the right of reproduction in whole or in part in any form.
Little Bee Books is a trademark of Bonnier Publishing USA, and associated colophon is a trademark of Bonnier Publishing USA.

Library of Congress Cataloging-in-Publication Data
Names: Reed, Melody, author.
Title: Starstruck / by Melody Reed; illustrated by Émilie Pépin.
Description: First edition. | New York, NY: Little Bee Books, [2018].
Series: The Major Eights; #4 | Summary: "When Becca finds out about her school's free throw competition, she is ready to put her basketball skills to the test! And if she wins, she'll get to meet her favorite basketball player! But after a series of bad practices, her nerves start to get the best of her. Can the Major Eights help Becca regain her confidence and meet her hero?"—Provided by publisher.
Identifiers: LCCN 2018005683 | Subjects: | CYAC: Basketball—Fiction. | Contests—Fiction. | Friendship—Fiction. | Bands (Music)—Fiction. | BISAC: JUVENILE FICTION / Readers / Chapter Books. | JUVENILE FICTION / Performing Arts / Music. | JUVENILE FICTION / Girls & Women.
Classification: LCC PZ7.1.R428 St 2018 | DDC [Fic]—dc23
LC record available at https://lccn.loc.gov/2018005683

Printed in the United States of America LAK 1118
ISBN 978-1-4998-0590-1 (hc)
First Edition 10 9 8 7 6 5 4 3 2 1
ISBN 978-1-4998-0589-5 (pb)
First Edition 10 9 8 7 6 5 4 3 2
littlebeebooks.com
bonnierpublishingusa.com

THE MAJOR EIGHTS

STARSTRUCK

by Melody Reed
illustrated by Émilie Pépin

little bee books

CONTENTS

THE WALL OF FAME

As soon as Mom parked the car in front of our house, I undid my seat belt and threw open the door. I was running late for band practice with the Major Eights.

"Becca," Mom called. "Don't forget to take your trash."

"But, Mom," I said, "I'm late!"

"Your friends can wait two minutes."

My big brothers, Lucas and Manny, hopped out of the car.

"Whoops," said Manny. "I can't forget this!" He grabbed a gold basketball trophy from the backseat.

Lucas whooped. "Uh-huh. Two more trophies for the Wall!"

I frowned at my brothers. "Hey, my team was pretty close!" But Lucas and Manny were almost inside the house and didn't hear me.

I wadded up my hot dog wrapper in my fist and ran after them.

From the front door, I heard Jasmine playing chords in my family's garage. Scarlet sang scales. Maggie played a solo on the drum set. I quickly disposed of my trash and raced to the garage.

My family doesn't park our cars in our garage. A shag rug covers the floor. An old sofa sits against the far wall. My oldest brother, Tony, has an old guitar that sits in one corner. Along another whole wall runs my family's Wall of Fame. It has tons of awards and trophies. All of them belong to my three big brothers.

"I'm here!" I announced to my friends. "What did I miss?"

"Hey, Becca!" said Maggie. "You're just in time!"

"Is basketball season over now?" asked Scarlet.

"How was your last game?" asked Jasmine.

"Yeah, it was our last game," I said. "It went great! We didn't win, though."

"Maybe next year," said Jasmine.

I nodded. I took my place, trying not to look at the Wall of Fame.

Lucas and Manny had already added their new trophies to it. The only thing I had up there was a poster. It wasn't signed, like my brothers' posters on the Wall. But it was a picture of Lucy "the Leaper" Landon. Lucy was the best point guard in the world. She played on the basketball team at Center State University. I got to see her play a few months ago.

"Are you guys ready to practice?" Jasmine asked. "I think 'Take My Shot' is really sounding good. This should be the one we play at Scarlet's cousin's party next weekend."

"Yeah!" said Scarlet.

"Totally!" said Maggie.

"Sure," I said, still gazing over at the poster.

My friends waited.

"Oh, right." I grabbed a guitar pick. "*I* start this one."

I played the first chords.

Scarlet sang, "It's time . . . to take my shot. . . ."

As I strummed, I continued to stare at the poster.

I didn't have any trophies on the Wall—yet. But with basketball season over, I wouldn't be adding any to the Wall soon. But a signed poster would be even *better* than a trophy.

If only I could find a way to meet Lucy.

THE FREE
THROW *FUNTEST*

"Remember!" our teacher shouted, bending his wrist over his head. "Like this!" Mr. Akers was demonstrating free throws in gym class that week.

I held the ball over my head. Then I snapped my wrist. The ball flew toward the hoop.

Swish! The ball went in, hitting nothing but net.

"Yes!" I yelled.

At the hoop next to me, Robby Thompson smirked. He flicked his wrist and hit a free throw too.

"Ha!" He pumped his fist in the air. "I'm the best free throw shooter ever!"

His friends thumped him on the back.

I shot again, and the ball bounced off the rim.

Robby locked eyes with me. Then he moved to the side of the basket and tossed another ball toward the net.

Another *swish!* for Robby Thompson.

He put up another shot, and missed.

I tried not to smile. My coach says that's poor sportsmanship.

"Okay," said Mr. Akers. "Eighteen out of twenty for Robby. Nice work." He made a note on his clipboard.

Robby looked pleased with himself.

I ignored him and shot my last ball. It bounced off the rim again.

I groaned.

"And fourteen for Becca. Not bad."
Mr. Akers made another note. "Okay,
circle up! I've got an announcement to
make before recess. Next week, we're
going to have a special assembly,"
he said. "The whole school is going
to have a free throw contest. Anyone
can enter. Whoever makes the most
baskets out of twenty will win. It's
called the Free Throw *Fun*test."

He waited for everyone to laugh, but we just stared straight ahead, not getting the joke.

"You know," he said, "because it's a *contest* and it's *fun*. Get it?"

I threw my hand up. "Mr. Akers? Is there a prize for the winner?"

He chuckled. "That's the best part. Whoever wins gets to meet and have their picture taken with Lucy Landon!"

"*What?!*" I exclaimed. "Are you *serious*?!"

But Robby just put his chin up in the air. "Huh, I already know her," he muttered.

Mr. Akers got his pen out. "Okay, who wants to enter?"

I threw a fist in the air. "Me!"

"Yeah, I guess." Robby raised his hand meekly.

I lifted an eyebrow. "If you don't care about meeting Lucy Landon, you don't have to enter the contest."

He shrugged. "Well, at least I can beat you again. That's always fun."

I put my hands on my hips. "You think you can beat *me*?" I asked. "When a meeting with Lucy 'the Leaper' Landon is the prize? No way!"

One of Robby's friends stepped up. "Robby's good, Becca. He has a private coach."

I frowned. "You have a private coach?" I asked. "For basketball?"

Robby grinned. "That's right," he said. "And he'll help me win. It's what my dad pays him to do."

Well, coach or no coach, I was going to win that contest. I could already see my poster of Lucy—now *signed*—on our Wall. No way was Robby Thompson going to steal Lucy Landon from me!

MAJOR EIGHTS TO THE RESCUE!

After the bell, Mr. Akers dismissed us for recess. The blacktop flooded with kids. Balls bounced and swings creaked.

I walked over to check out a basketball.

"Hi, Becca!" Scarlet got in line behind me. "What's up?"

Jasmine and Maggie joined us.

"What are you guys doing for recess?" Maggie asked. "Kevin asked me to play kickball with him and his friends. Wanna come?"

"Can't," I answered. "I have to practice."

"Let me guess," said Scarlet. "Free throws? We heard about the contest."

"And that player you like is coming, right?" asked Jasmine.

I grinned and nodded. "I absolutely need to win," I said. "I *have* to meet Lucy the Leaper!"

"Do you really think you can win?" asked Scarlet.

Across the playground, Robby put up a shot with a basketball he'd already checked out.

I balled up my fists and scowled. "Of course I can."

"Maybe we can help!" said Maggie.

"Yeah," said Scarlet. "Not that you need it. But we could all enter too."

"And if one of us wins, we could give the prize to you!" said Maggie.

I smiled. "Thanks. That's really nice, you guys."

"You'll, um . . . have to give us some tips, though," said Jasmine. "Maybe during our next band practice?"

I brightened up at that. "You mean we could shoot some hoops at the park? And *then* band practice?"

"If it'll help," Jasmine said.

"Yeah!" Maggie agreed.

"You bet!" Scarlet said.

I grinned. If I had my friends behind me, nothing could stop me!

A PRIVATE COACH

After school, I dropped my backpack in the hallway, grabbed a basketball out of the closet, and raced to my room. I put on my gray sweats and a black T-shirt with a basketball logo on it. I looked in the mirror. *Perfect.*

"Mom?" I called. I wandered out of my room, looking for her.

Lucas strolled out of the kitchen, taking an ape-sized bite out of an apple.

"Where's Mom?" I asked.

"She took Manny to an ortho appointment." He raised his eyebrows. "*I'm* in charge."

"Great," I said. "Well, I'm meeting my friends at the park."

"Mom didn't say you could go to the park."

"Lucas, I *have* to go to the park. I have to practice!"

"What for?"

"There's a contest at school. I need to win it."

He shrugged. "Okay, okay. I'll be a nice big brother. I'll walk you over."

I exhaled. "Thanks."

We slammed the door behind us.

"What are you practicing anyway?" Lucas asked.

"Free throws." I dribbled the ball as we walked.

"Is this because the Leaper's coming to your school?"

"How did you know?"

Lucas eyed the ball. "The whole town's talking about it. My friend Jake's little brother is in the contest too."

"*Fun*test," I said. "Who's his little brother?"

"Robby Thompson."

"Oh." I set my jaw. "Well, I'm going to beat him."

"I don't know, sis. Their dad works for the Center State athletic department. He hires private coaches for his kids for every sport they play. If Robby's anything like Jake, he'll be tough to beat."

I furrowed my brow. "Why does everyone keep saying that? Having a private coach doesn't mean Robby's better than me."

"No, but it *does* mean he'll have an edge."

"What's that mean?"

"It means he'll have an advantage over other competitors."

"Oh."

I bounced the ball again and Lucas stole it away.

"Hey!" I cried.

"C'mon," he said, weaving the ball around and through his legs. "Try to take it back!"

I bent my knees to get low to the ground. Just as he brought the basketball around his hip, I slapped it to the ground. Then I whirled around so I was between him and the ball.

"What?!" he yelled.

I grinned and ran to the basketball courts with the ball.

"Hey! That's traveling!" Lucas called.

I giggled, out of breath, as I arrived at the courts first. And then I stopped short.

My friends were waiting for me beneath one hoop.

But at the other hoop, a kid shot free throws near a guy in a warm-up suit.

It was Robby Thompson and his private coach.

PRACTICE MAKES PERFECT

Lucas elbowed me. "I'll be doing pull-ups over on the monkey bars. Call me if you need something."

Scarlet jerked her head in Robby's direction. "They said we could use this hoop," she told me.

"We don't need their permission," I growled. "It's a public park."

"Yeah," said Maggie. "But they were here first. Anyway, we're ready for you to give us tips."

I got behind the free throw line. "Okay, so you stand here. Then . . . you just . . . shoot!" I showed them how to stand, bend their bodies, and launch the ball toward the basket. *Swish!*

"Nice job!" my friends said, cheering.

Robby and his coach were doing dribbling drills. When Robby caught me watching them, he made a face at me.

I ignored him and turned back to my friends. "Okay, Scarlet, you try." I handed the ball to her.

Scarlet bit her lip. "Are you sure I'm supposed to be this far back?"

"Yeah," I said. "Just do what I did."

But Scarlet didn't. "I think I'm too close to Robby and his coach," she said. She moved up—*way* up—until she was right beneath the basket. The ball bounced off the rim and back down to her. Scarlet shrieked and leaped out of the way.

This was going to be harder than I'd thought.

And it didn't get any better. Maggie would only shoot underhanded. And Jasmine couldn't get the ball high enough, no matter what I told her.

"Okay," I told Jasmine again. "Like this, remember?" I shot another imaginary basket.

Jasmine nodded. But then she shot the ball *forward* instead of up. Scarlet and Maggie dove out of the way of the flying basketball.

I slapped my forehead.

"Hey," Robby called. "How's it going, Becca?"

"Great, thanks." I pasted a fake smile on my face.

Robby took a sip from his water bottle. "I'm just having a coaching session," he said. "With my private coach, Larry."

"Larry?" I swallowed. "As in Larry Rivers? From Center State?"

"Yep." Robby beamed. His coach was a star player in college.

I tried not to look impressed. "Well, we're practicing too. So . . . you'd better watch out."

Robby just laughed.

We can do this, I told myself. *Practice makes perfect.*

My friends gathered around me.

"I don't know if this is a good idea, Becca," said Scarlet.

"Me either," said Maggie.

"We're pretty awful," said Jasmine.

"You guys just need practice," I insisted. "And so do I."

"Okay," Maggie said. "You practice, Becca, and we'll get the ball for you."

I aimed for the backboard and shot the ball. It bounced off and Maggie ran to get it.

"Didn't you say one hand is supposed to be behind the ball?" asked Scarlet.

I blinked. "Yeah."

Jasmine shook her head. "Hmm . . . Maybe when you shoot too quickly, you put your hand in the wrong spot. Try slowing down—like how you were showing us."

Maggie handed me the ball.

This time I pretended I was teaching someone how to shoot. The ball went in!

I grinned. "Hey, you guys were right!"

Across the court, Robby made a basket too.

Frowning, I took another shot. This one didn't even hit the backboard. Scarlet ran after it.

My shoulders slumped.

"Why don't you ask your mom to get a coach for you?" asked Jasmine.

I hadn't even thought of that. "Do you think she would?"

"It doesn't hurt to ask!" Scarlet said with a grin.

I watched Robby's coach adjust Robby's form. Then Robby shot a perfect basket.

If my friends could help my form, a coach could help even more. Maybe it wasn't practice that made you perfect at something. Maybe the right coach did.

MAYBE NEXT YEAR

That night, my brothers all left the table right after dinner.

I scooped up their dirty plates without being asked. "So, Mom," I said.

"Uh-oh," said Dad. "She wants something, Rosita."

Mom loaded the plates into the dishwasher. "What is it, sweetie?"

"Hey, how's your band doing?" Dad interrupted. He rinsed out a glass. "I heard you guys practicing in the garage the other day. Sounds good!"

"Thanks," I said. "We've been working on a new song. It's for a party this weekend." I handed Mom more dishes. "So, Mom . . ." I passed her two glasses. "You know how Lucy Landon is the best point guard ever? Well, I might get to meet her!"

Mom blinked. "Wow. That's wonderful, sweetie."

"Yeah," I said. "All I have to do is win a free throw contest. It's Friday afternoon at a special assembly."

"That's great!" said Dad. "You should have no problem, then."

"Well," I said, "that's the thing. See, I'm good, but I'm not *that* good. One kid I know . . . has a private coach. Just for basketball. Isn't that cool?"

Mom and Dad exchanged a look.

Dad smirked. "So that's where this is going."

I turned to Mom. "Wouldn't it be great if I had a private coach to help me win the contest?"

Mom smiled. "Sweetie, private coaches cost a lot of money. You play several sports. We can't hire private coaches for all of them."

"But I don't need private coaches for everything. Only for basketball. Just this one time for the contest."

"It's not just about the money, Becca," said Dad. "It's also about the time."

A lump settled in my stomach. This was not going well.

"Your dad's right. I already have a lot to do every day. I don't have time to take you to private lessons."

"I can take myself. We could do it at the park like Robby Thompson."

"Robby Thompson?" Dad added. "The kid you're talking about is a Thompson? Becca, his dad is a coach for the university. He knows people in athletics we don't."

I turned back to Mom with pleading eyes. "Please, Mom?"

"I'm sorry, sweetie. Maybe next year." She closed the dishwasher and it hummed.

But next year, I thought, *there won't be a chance to meet Lucy.*

I was going to have to figure out something else.

SNAP!

For the next week, I practiced free throws every day.

The day before the contest and the birthday party, I strummed the last chord of "Take My Shot." "This song rocks!" I announced.

"I think we play it even better than 'Fox Pox,'" said Jasmine.

"My cousin's going to love it!" said Scarlet. "I can't wait till her birthday party!"

I stared at the floor. "I wish I felt as ready for the contest," I said with a sigh. "The only way I'm going to meet Lucy is if I win."

"Let's do the song one more time," Maggie said.

I played the opening chord. But I hit the last string too hard. There was a sharp *twang*. "Aaaa!" I shrieked.

"What happened?!" asked Jasmine.

Scarlet and Maggie rushed over to me.

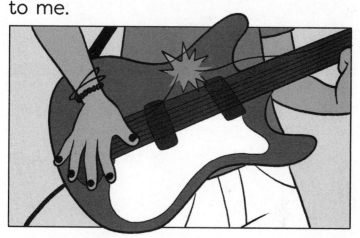

I stared at my guitar. I had broken one of the strings!

"Can you fix it?" asked Jasmine.

I swallowed and shook my head. "I need to replace it."

"Do you have more?" asked Maggie.

I shook my head again. "I'm pretty sure I'm all out."

"But we have to play tomorrow! What are you going to do?" asked Scarlet.

My chest felt heavy. I jerked my head toward the old guitar in the corner. "I can use Tony's, I guess."

"He won't mind?"

"Nah," I said. "He has two others. He hasn't used that one in forever."

But that guitar was
old and too big for
me. And worst of all,
it was bright red.

This song had been the one thing
going right this week. Now I had to
use a guitar I didn't like for it. And I
still had to beat Robby Thompson at
free throws.

That was feeling harder and harder
to do.

Tweeeeet! Mr. Akers blew his whistle.

The Free Throw Funtest was off to a slow start. A line of fifty or so kids snaked along one side of the gym, which had been decorated with colorful streamers for the event. The rest of the school filled up the bleachers to watch.

The contestants would each get five shots during the first round. We had to make at least three to go on to the next round. There would be three rounds total. So far, nobody had made three baskets.

The next kid stepped up to the free throw line.

Lucy the Leaper stood next to Mr. Akers and clapped for each kid. She was even taller than I'd thought she'd be. Her curls weren't in a ponytail like when she played. Instead, they fanned out and seemed to float around her face.

I shook out my hands as I waited for my turn.

Did Lucy make everyone feel as nervous as I did?

The rest of the Major Eights waved from the front row of the bleachers. They'd already had their turns at the free throw line. They sat with our instruments, ready for my mom to take us to the party after the contest. Tony's awful red guitar was among them.

Robby leaned forward in line. "Ready for me to beat you?" he taunted.

I rolled my eyes.

"Hey," Robby whispered. "Guess what? My dad organized this contest."

"Huh?"

"Yeah. He's the one who asked Lucy to come. Because we know her, you know."

I folded my arms. "So what?"

Robby smirked. "So she only came to see *me*."

I turned my back to him. Did Lucy really just want to see Robby, no matter who won?

Tweeet! "Next up, Becca Rodriguez, third grade," Mr. Akers called.

The sound of my own name jolted me out of my thoughts. I stepped up to the free throw line. My hands shook anxiously as I took the ball from Mr. Akers.

"All right, let's go!" Lucy clapped.

For a second, I froze up.

But then I heard my friends cheering.

"You can do it!" shouted Jasmine.

"Go for it, Becca!" called Maggie.

"Woo-hoo!" whooped Scarlet.

I took my first shot. *Swish!*

I grinned. The teachers behind the hoop bounced me a second ball. I dribbled twice, then took aim.

It bounced off the rim.

So did my third.

I took a deep breath, then shot the fourth.

Come on, I told myself. *Just one more to make it to the next round.*

I launched the ball into the air. Nothing but net!

The crowd cheered and clapped loudly for me.

I ran over to the other Major Eights.

"You did it!" they all shouted.

"Well, I made it to the next round!" I exclaimed.

During the next round, Robby made four out of five baskets, just like he did in the first round. He threw his fists in the air.

Ah, great, I thought.

My breaths came fast as I stepped up for my turn. But I got three out of five, qualifying for the final round!

I glanced at Lucy when I made the last basket. She was smiling! Lucy "the Leaper" Landon was cheering for *me*!

Then suddenly, I remembered. I'd forgotten to bring the poster!

Oh, no. No, no, no.

Now, even if I won, I still wouldn't have anything to add to the Wall at home after all.

I had to think of something—and it had to be fast!

LUCY "THE LEAPER" LANDON

LANDON

36

I racked my brain. I had to find a way to get my hands on that poster!

"What's wrong?" asked Maggie.

"I forgot the poster," I said. "I don't have anything to get signed if I win." I slumped down onto the bench.

Jasmine frowned. "There must be something else Lucy could sign. Maybe your shoe?"

"Maybe," I said. I tried to picture a shoe hanging on the Wall. I didn't think that would work too well.

Tweet! Mr. Akers announced the final contestants. It was down to just me and Robby.

Mr. Akers told us we'd have ten shots each, to finish out our twenty. Robby already had hit eight out of ten and I only had six.

Robby turned to me. "I'm already ahead. Looks like I'm gonna win."

"I'll get more than you *this* round," I said. "Just watch me."

He smirked. "No way."

I turned, fuming, as we lined up behind free throw lines at opposite ends of the gym.

Lucy grinned and clapped for us. She was awfully nice. She didn't seem like she would be friends with someone like Robby Thompson.

Mr. Akers puffed into his whistle. He tossed balls to both Robby and me.

"Go, Becca!" shouted my friends.

My mom had arrived too and was sitting next to my friends. She gave me a thumbs-up.

I put up my first shot. It bounced wildly off the rim. My shoulders sagged a little, and I tried not to picture Robby sinking ball after ball behind me.

I shot some more, missing a few.

Lucy was watching Robby. She nodded and clapped. But then her face turned to me, and she smiled.

I shot my ball toward the basket again. Remembering what my friends had said, I took it nice and slow. *Swish!*

Lucy cheered!

My cheeks burned.

Mr. Akers quieted the crowd, announcing that Robby and I were tied with only one shot left each!

I tried not to think of him behind me.

Balancing the ball above my head, I bent my knees. Then I jumped and snapped my wrist.

The ball sailed through the air. It circled the rim. And just when it looked like it would fall into the hoop, it rolled out, falling to the ground. I missed.

But the crowd cheered.

For a second, I was confused. Then I realized they weren't cheering for me.

Robby had made his basket. He'd won the contest.

"And the winner is Robby Thompson!" announced Mr. Akers. "By one basket!"

The crowd cheered louder.

Lucy smiled as she walked over to Robby. She put an arm around him and they posed for a picture.

I couldn't watch. I dragged myself back to the bleachers to sit with my mom and the Major Eights.

"You did so well out there, sweetie," said Mom.

"You'll always be a star to us," said Scarlet.

I sighed. "Thanks, guys."

The crowd was noisy as kids chatted and stood up to leave.

Maggie pulled out her drumsticks. She started a beat on the bench as we waited.

I pulled out Tony's guitar. "I guess I could tune up before we get to the party." I plucked strings and turned pegs. As I tuned, I wondered what Robby would have Lucy sign.

Then someone tapped me on the shoulder. "Um, excuse me?"

I spun around.

"Are you the Major Eights?" asked Lucy Landon.

THE AUTOGRAPH

"Are you *actually* the Major Eights?" Lucy asked again.

My mouth fell open, but I somehow managed to nod.

Lucy's hands flew to her face. "I can't believe it! I saw you guys at the Battle of the Bands. You really wrote that song yourselves?"

I nodded again.

"How old are you?" Lucy asked.

"Um . . . eight," I said.

"You know, the Major *Eights*," added Jasmine from behind us.

"Oh, man!" said Lucy. She waved to the photographer across the gym. He ran over to us.

I shook my head. "Oh, but—I didn't win the free throw contest."

Lucy squatted in front of me. "You've got it all wrong," she said. "*You're* the one who's famous. I'm a big fan of your group. Can I get my picture taken with you?"

I giggled. "*Me?*"

She nodded.

"Um, YES!" I said.

Lucy put her arm around my shoulders. I still had Tony's guitar on, so I acted like I was playing it. Lucy made a "wow" face and pointed at me. The photographer snapped the picture.

"Hey, guys. Come over here!" I called to my friends.

They climbed down the bleachers. Lucy knelt in front of us. My mom jumped in behind the photographer. She grinned as she snapped pictures of us on her phone.

When we were done, Lucy turned to me. "Hey, you're pretty good at free throws. Do you play on a team?"

"Yeah," I said. "Our season just ended."

"How about a private coaching session sometime?" she asked. "If it's okay with your mom."

My jaw dropped. "Are you serious?"

"Yeah, for sure!" she said. "I'll give your mom my number. Before I go, do you have anything you'd like me to autograph?"

I looked around for something. If only I hadn't forgotten the poster! I shrugged.

Scarlet whispered, "Have her sign the guitar!"

Lucy pulled out a marker. "I can do that."

My mouth went dry. I didn't have anything on the Wall. But none of my brothers had a *signed guitar*. This would be way, *way* better than any poster! I glanced at my mom, who nodded that it was okay.

"Yes!" I shrieked and held the guitar while Lucy signed it.

Her autograph was big and messy.
"Wow," I said.

Lucy winked. "Oh, cool. Red's my
favorite color."

"Yeah?" I looked down at Tony's
guitar. Maybe a red guitar wasn't so
bad after all.

"Hey," said Lucy. "Will you play me out?"

"We'd love to!" said Jasmine. She plugged her keyboard into her amp, and I did the same with Tony's guitar. Maggie hit her sticks together for the first beats. "Five, six, seven, eight!" she called.

I rocked my first chord. Then strummed two more.

But where was Scarlet? She was supposed to come in soon.

Suddenly, Scarlet's voice echoed around the gym. She'd grabbed Mr. Akers's mic!

"It's time . . . to take my shot. . . ." she sang.

I strummed two more chords.

Mr. Akers turned toward us as the music got louder. He wasn't even mad. He was laughing!

"Can't tell . . . what I've got . . ." sang Scarlet.

The gym was still half full. Kids and teachers stopped to watch. Suddenly, *everyone* was watching us play!

Across the gym, Lucy stood with Robby and his dad. She was grinning and clapping. Robby's dad was too. I saw Robby roll his eyes. But then I could tell he got into it when his foot started tapping along.

When my friends and I finished the song, the whole gym cheered. Scarlet skipped back over to us.

The four Major Eights stood in a line. We took a bow all together.

"Major Eights forever!" I cried.

"Totally! At least until we turn nine," Scarlet said.

Maggie frowned. "I guess we'll have to come up with a new name then."

Jasmine shook her head. "We started this band when we were eight. That will always be true."

"Good point," I said. "Major Eights forever!"

My friends grinned. "That's right. Major Eights forever!"

Read on for a sneak peek from the fifth book in THE MAJOR EiGHTS series, *The New Bandmate.*

THE MAJOR EIGHTS

THE NEW BANDMATE

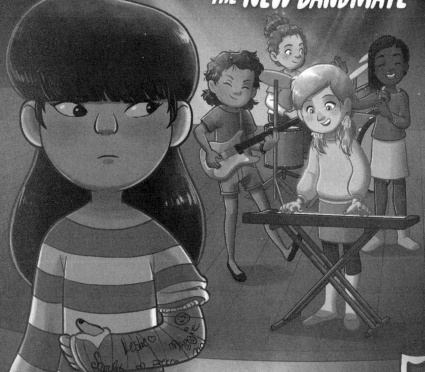

"In third place is . . . Jasmine Li!"

I blinked. Had he just said my name?

Sure enough, the judge in charge of the piano competition waved me up onstage. Three trophies sat on the table behind him. He handed me the shortest one.

"Thanks," I murmured, trying to smile. I'd practiced every day for a month. I really thought I had a shot at first place this time. Oh, well. At least I'd won something.

"And in second place is . . . Nate Stevens!"

A boy rushed up from the back of the room. His family cheered for him.

Becca, Maggie, and Scarlet smiled at

me from the front row. My parents and my brother, Nick, sat next to them. It was a Saturday. The room at the community center was packed. The regional competition is a big deal every year.

The judge gave Nate his trophy, then picked up the last one. The biggest one. "And finally, first place goes to . . . Leslie Miller!"

Leslie's blond pigtails bounced as she skipped up the steps. She shook the judge's free hand. Her grin stretched from ear to ear. The trophy was so big, she had to hold it with both of her hands.

Leslie had won another piano competition.

But I forced myself to smile anyway. "Good job," I told her.

"You, too!" Leslie beamed. "Your piece was nice."

I smiled for real. Staying mad at Leslie for long was hard to do.

Becca put a hand on my shoulder. "I'm sorry, Jas," she said. "I know you worked hard for this."

"Really good job," said Scarlet. Maggie nodded next to her.

"Thanks, guys." I smiled at my friends.

"See you tomorrow for practice?" Maggie asked.

I grinned. "That's right! We have the show at Tony's next week." Tony's Tacos is a restaurant downtown. Tony, the owner, had heard our band play and asked us to play a song for his customers sometime. "I'll see you guys tomorrow!"

"Good job, honey," said my mom.

"Proud of you, Jasmine," said my dad.

"Hey, Jas," said Nick. "Next time, maybe you should wear pigtails."

I frowned. "Ha-ha."

"No, I'm serious," he said. "Leslie keeps winning competitions and you don't. Either she has magic hair or she's just better at piano than you."

"Nick," warned my dad, "I believe that's enough."

I balled up my fists. "She is *not* better than me!"

My parents scooted us all out of the building. Some of the kids from the competition were horsing around on the community center playground.

Leslie hung from the high bar. "Jasmine,"

she called. "Come play with us!"

I zipped over to the playground and pulled up on the bar next to Leslie.

"Watch how far I can go!" she said. She swung off the bar and let go, landing on her feet.

"I bet I can go farther," I said. I swung my body to pick up speed.

But just as I was about to let go, one of my hands slipped. I crashed to the ground.

A sharp pain ran up my arm.

Leslie ran over. "Oh, no! Jasmine, are you okay?"

I sat up. My arm hurt so much I couldn't think straight. I tried to move my fingers, but I couldn't. "No," I gasped. "I don't think so!"